TOM FOOLERY

by Curtis Parkinson · illustrated by Cathy Bobak

Bradbury Press · New York

Maxwell Macmillan Canada   Toronto
Maxwell Macmillan International
New York   Oxford   Singapore   Sydney

Bradbury Press
Macmillan Publishing Company
866 Third Avenue
New York, NY 10022

Maxwell Macmillan Canada, Inc.
1200 Eglinton Avenue East
Suite 200
Don Mills, Ontario M3C 3N1

Macmillan Publishing Company is part of
the Maxwell Communication Group of Companies.

First Edition
Printed and bound in Hong Kong by
South China Printing Company (1988) Ltd.
10 9 8 7 6 5 4 3 2 1

The text of this book is set in 18 point Monticello.
The illustrations are rendered in watercolor.
Book design by Julie Quan

Library of Congress Cataloging-in-Publication Data
Parkinson, Curtis.
Tom Foolery / by Curtis Parkinson ; illustrated by Cathy Bobak.—
1st ed.
p.   cm.
Summary: Tom Foolery, a curious cat, falls off Captain Andy's boat
and has exciting adventures on a nearby island.
ISBN 0-02-770025-9
[1. Cats—Fiction.   2. Islands—Fiction.]   I. Bobak, Cathy, ill.
II. Title.
PZ7.P23918To   1993
[E]—dc20   92-7852

For Megan and Lindsay, and Marmalade

C. P.

For Angelo

C. B.

Tom Foolery lived on a boat. It had sails for the wind to fill, an anchor to keep it still, and netting all around to keep Tom from falling off.

But Tom liked to chew things, and one day he chewed a hole right through the netting.

When Captain Andy saw the hole, he exclaimed,
"Tom Foolery! Now, don't you go near that
until it is mended."

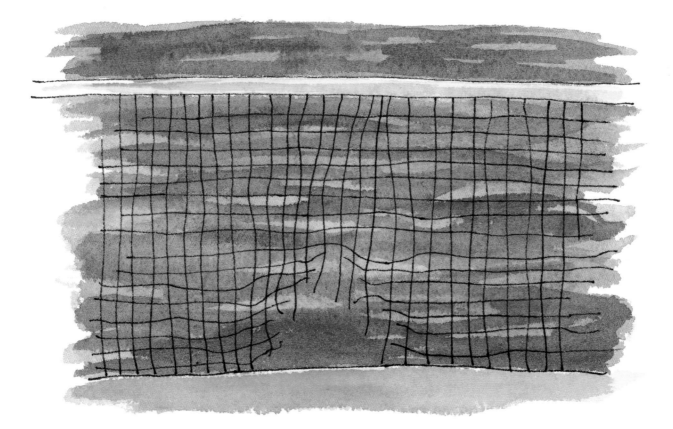

But late that night Tom heard a fish splash,
and he leaned out just a little to have a look.

Another fish splashed, and he leaned a little
farther…and a little farther. Suddenly a wave
rocked the boat. Tom lost his balance and fell
into the water—*kersplash!*

Captain Andy and his daughter, Megan,
were sound asleep in the cabin below. They didn't
hear the splash when Tom fell in. He meowed
and meowed, but his calls were lost in the wind.

When no one came to rescue him, Tom
swam as hard as he could toward the shore. He
swam and he swam, and at last his feet touched
the bottom.

Tom staggered onto the beach
and lay down on the warm sand
to rest and to lick himself dry.

After a while it started to rain, so he looked for a tree to shelter under. He didn't know that the pelicans roosted in that tree, and they didn't want to share it with anyone!

Tom got such a fright that he ran into the woods, up a big hill, and down the other side.

He didn't stop until he was a long way from the pelicans—away on the other side of the island. Then he hid under a bush and stayed there for the rest of the night.

Megan always got up early in the morning to give Tom Foolery his breakfast. But this morning he didn't come when she called.

She and Captain Andy looked in every hiding place on the boat.

Then they rowed their little dinghy to the beach to search the shore.

They called, "Tom Foolery, Tom Foolery," again and again, but there was no answer. So they decided to sail around to the other side of the island to look for him there.

Meanwhile Tom Foolery had fallen asleep
under the bush where he had been hiding.

When he woke up he was very hungry. He set off
back up the big hill to find the boat and his breakfast.

Labels within the illustration: TOM'S BOAT; TOM FOOLERY'S BUSH; BIG HILL; PELICAN TREE

So when Megan and Captain Andy arrived
at the bush, Tom wasn't there...

and when Tom arrived back at the beach,
the boat wasn't there—only some laughing gulls
crying, "Ha, ha ha ha."

Tom wandered about the island looking for Megan and Captain Andy. As he wandered he began to smell something delicious.

He followed the delicious smell until he came to a cottage. Something very good was cooking in the kitchen.

Tom badly wanted to get into that kitchen, but a dog lived there.

He had to wait for just the
right moment...

to scoot in the door.

There was a lot
to see and do.

The lady with the apron gave Tom a big
helping of stew from the pot on the stove.

Afterward he curled up for a nap, purring contentedly, and thought, "This is such a nice place, maybe I could stay here."

But then he dreamt about Megan and Captain Andy
and his home, and he knew he had to find them again.

So Tom scratched
at the door until the lady
with the apron let him
out, but...

he had forgotten about the dog,

who wanted to play a game of chase.

Tom raced to a tree and
climbed to a high branch
while the dog barked and
barked below.

The barking of the dog
echoed across the island.

When Megan and Captain Andy heard
it, they hurried to see if Tom was there.
They arrived just as the lady with the apron was
rescuing him from the tree.

Megan hugged him and hugged him.

Then they all had tea and cake
in the cottage, except for the dog, who had
biscuits, and Tom, who had some more stew.

Tom Foolery